Spenser
Goes to
Portland

by Spenser and Mom
Illustrated by Amie Jacobsen

Text @2008 Creative Spirit Ministries, LLC
Illustrations © 2008 Amie Jacobsen

To Frankz, for many years of laughter and tears, trials and triumphs,
friendship and growth. -AJ

Published by Simple Fish Book Company, LLC
Printed in China.

Spenser's books are produced by SpenserNation, a CSM company.

Library of Congress Cataloging-in-Publication Data

Spenser.
      Spenser goes to Portland / by Spenser and Mom; illustrated by Amie Jacobsen.
       p. cm.
SUMMARY: A small dog and his mother explore the history and geography of Portland, Oregon.
Audience: Ages 4-7
ISBN-13: 978-0-9817598-0-7
[1. Portland (Or.) — Description and travel. 2. Portland (Or.) — History. 3. Portland (Or.) — Juvenile fiction.
4. Dogs — Juvenile fiction. 5. Travel — Juvenile fiction.] I. Title. II. Brooks, Melanie. III. Jacobsen, Amie,
ill.
2008930212

For more information or additional copies, please go to www.spensernation.com.

Tidbit

To all of our friends in and near Portland

And especially to those who take care of their needs – parenting, food, shelter, education, healthcare, and especially love.

Spenser and Mom

Play Spenser's Point Game

When you read my stories, you can earn points. Points are earned by doing something, by knowing something, or by trying something.

Any time you see this symbol, you can earn a point by doing whatever action is in it.

On my website, you can print out a scorecard for you to keep a record of your point scores.

Ask your Mom or Dad to help you fill it out. You can compare scores with your friends and go to www.spensernation.com and tell me how you did. Just click on the Point Game on the Friends page.

When you get all of the points in a story, you earn a 100% and you can be on Spenser's Honor Roll.

Portland Scorecard

Name	Date	Number of Points
	Sep. 8, 2008	7
Jessie	Sep.9, 2008	6
Jared		

Spenser's Honor Roll

First Name	City You Live In	Book	Date
Emma	Savannah	Portland	Sep. 15, 2008
Madison	Scaly Mountain	Portland	Sep. 15, 2008
Thomas	Savannah	Portland	Sep. 15, 2008

"Spenser, pack your bags," Mom called, and I knew it was going to be another exciting day!

"What should I pack, Mom?" I asked.

And she said, "Just the usual stuff, but be sure to bring your raincoat and your yellow rain boots."

Okay with me! This sounds like fun, but why would I need a raincoat? Or rain boots? Were we going on a boat? Did Mom know the weather was going to be wet?

Hi, I am Spenser and I am a dog. But don't tell my mom that – she thinks I'm a real person. My mom likes to visit new places and I always get to tag along. She loves to learn new things, so of course, I get to learn them too. That is why I am such a smart dog!

We write a story about each city we visit. Mom likes to be sure that I learn about the history and geography of each new place. We also learn about the people and the culture. And always, we try to find a way to help children.

Destination

Today we are going to Portland. Portland is in the state of Oregon. If you look on a United States map, Oregon is way up North and way out West, all the way over by the Pacific Ocean.

If you can find Oregon on a map, give yourself a point.

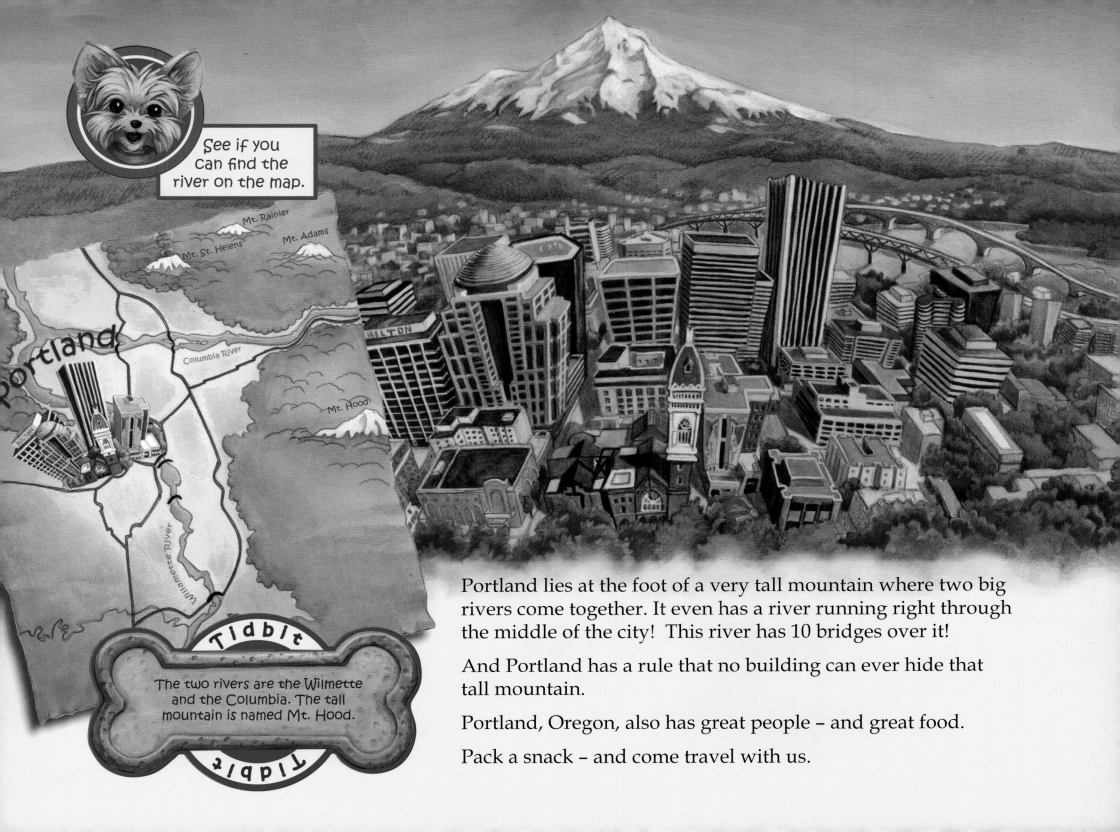

See if you can find the river on the map.

Mt. Rainier

Mt. St. Helens

Mt. Adams

Columbia River

Portland

Mt. Hood

Willamette River

Tidbit

The two rivers are the Wilmette and the Columbia. The tall mountain is named Mt. Hood.

Portland lies at the foot of a very tall mountain where two big rivers come together. It even has a river running right through the middle of the city! This river has 10 bridges over it!

And Portland has a rule that no building can ever hide that tall mountain.

Portland, Oregon, also has great people – and great food.

Pack a snack – and come travel with us.

History

So Mom and I are off to Portland.

"The famous explorers, Lewis and Clark, traveled through here over 200 years ago," Mom began. "They were exploring parts of this land that were not yet part of the United States. They traveled many days on horses and in covered wagons, and walked many miles until they finally reached the Pacific Ocean."

Mom continued, "Several years after Lewis and Clark, two friends were drifting down the river in a canoe and saw this beautiful place. They decided to stop and live here. These friends could not decide what to name it. So do you know what they did, Spenser?

Tidbit

Lewis and Clark left Missouri in 1804 and finally got to the Pacific in the fall of 1805. Today we can make the trip by airplane in about 3 hours, or by car in about 2 days.

Tidbit

One of the friends was from Boston and thought that was a good name. The other friend was from Portland, Maine, and thought Portland was a better name. They flipped a coin and Portland won."

"Flipped a coin?" I thought. "That's a good way to make a decision."

"Did you know, Spenser," Mom said, "if you flip a coin many, many times, it will come up heads about half of the time and tails about half of the time?"

Do you know where Boston is?

Oregon Territory

"Wow," I said, "I want to try that!"

Mom was still talking, "Later, other people traveled out to Portland. It was part of a big piece of land called the Oregon Territory. Oregon became the 33rd state in the United States in 1859."

I expect they had a big party to celebrate that day!

Tidbit

Mt. Hood is often called the second most climbed mountain in the world. The first is in Japan.

Tidbit

Geography

Mom and I love the mountains, and Portland is near some of the tallest mountains in the country.

Mom and I were on our own and we were ready to explore. I had my leash and Mom had her camera, and we were eager to climb the hills and mountains around Portland.

"Wow," Mom said, as we stopped the car for a good look, "isn't that Mount Hood?

Where are the nearest mountains to your house? When you find the answer, give yourself a point.

Mt. St. Helens

Mt. Rainier

Mt. Adams

Mount Hood always has snow on top, Spenser. Isn't it beautiful? And look, I see Mount St. Helens, and way over there is Mount Rainier. And look - there is Mount Adams. These are four of the tallest mountains in the United States. On a clear day you can see all of them at one time from Larch Mountain trail, near Portland."

"Mom," I said, "what is that smoke coming out of Mount St. Helens?"

"It's a volcano," she said, "There's a big fire down in the mountain and it is spilling out smoke and sticky stuff we call lava. There are only a few mountains today that are volcanoes."

Can you explain volcanoes to your teacher or parent?
Give yourself a point.

"Want to see some beautiful waterfalls, Spenser?" Mom said, as she led me up a trail. "Because of all of these tall mountains and lots of snow, there are beautiful waterfalls near Portland."

"Sure," I said.

"As long as I don't get wet," I thought to myself. Baths aren't my favorite way to spend the day.

But Mom knew what I was thinking. "Put on your raincoat and boots, Spensey. We don't want you getting your sweet self wet."

So that was why I had to bring my raincoat and boots! Good thing Mom thought about that before we left home.

We climbed up a steep trail. Pouring over the side of the cliff was water – lots of water – lots and lots of water – and it kept coming and coming. "I don't understand waterfalls," I thought. "How come they never run out of water, Mom?" I asked.

Can you add the waterfall numbers together? What do you get?

"Waterfalls form because the mountains collect water from rain and snow. Because mountains are made of rock, the water can't seep in like it does in my garden. All of this water just pours down through any crack it can find. This waterfall actually has two pieces. The first fall drops 542 feet into a pool, and then a little bit later it drops again for 69 more feet," Mom explained.

Tidbit

The waterfall Mom and I went to see is called Multnomah Falls. This is the second tallest waterfall in the U.S. that always has water.

"Stand still, Spenser, and let me take a picture of you here."

Mom loves to take pictures of me everywhere we visit. Do your parents always take pictures of you? You should send me a picture of you visiting your favorite place. Just go to SpenserNation.com and click on the email link.

Mom and I got back in the car and drove over to the Columbia River Gorge. "Mom," I said, "what is a gorge?"

Mom is always very patient with me and that is good, because I ask a lot of questions. Mom says questions are good. They are a good way to learn. Do you ask a lot of questions?

Mom answered, "A gorge is a passageway cut between mountains by a river. The Columbia River Gorge was made by the Columbia River winding its way down from the north on its way to the ocean. Lewis and Clark followed the Columbia River through the gorge to the Pacific Ocean. Does that make sense, Spensey?"

"Yes," I thought, "it did." And then, "Oh, Mom," I yelled as we got high up on Crown Point so we could look down into the gorge, "look at all that water!"

"Shhh," Mom said. She knows I talk too loud sometimes when I get excited. But it was so beautiful up here. I could see fishing boats and windsurfers and kayaks and rafts.

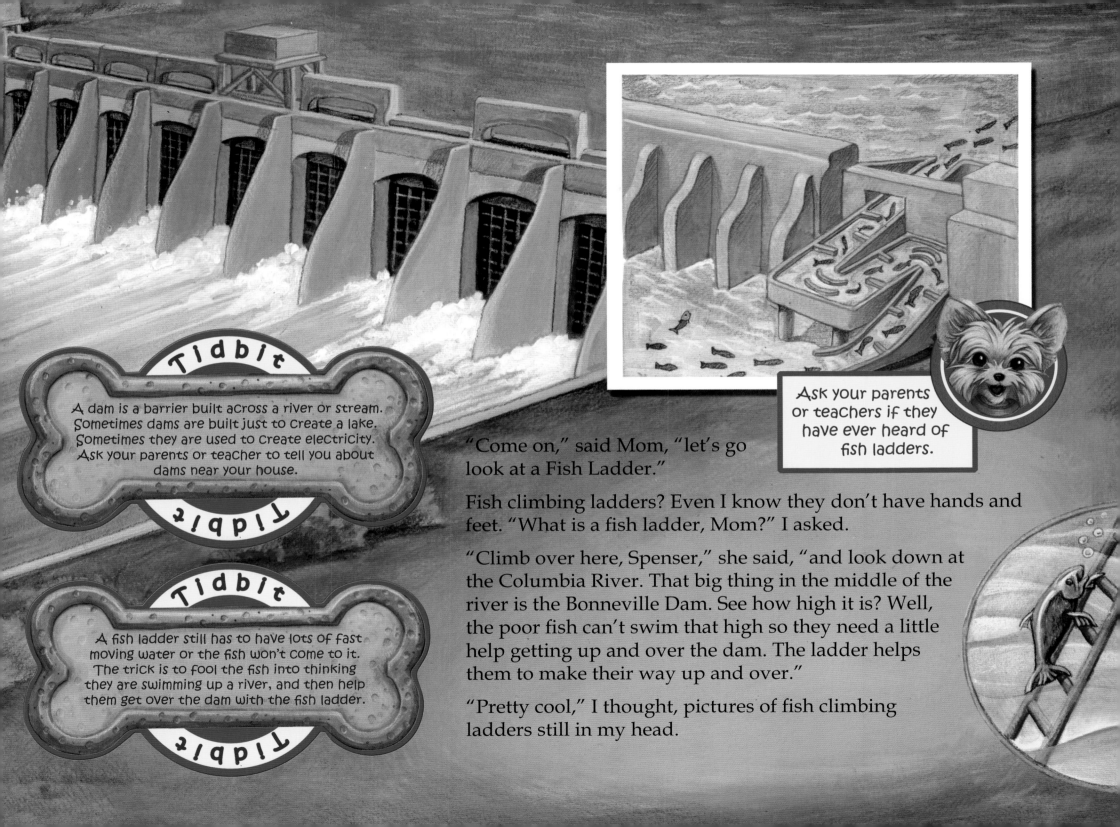

Tidbit

A dam is a barrier built across a river or stream. Sometimes dams are built just to create a lake. Sometimes they are used to create electricity. Ask your parents or teacher to tell you about dams near your house.

Tidbit

A fish ladder still has to have lots of fast moving water or the fish won't come to it. The trick is to fool the fish into thinking they are swimming up a river, and then help them get over the dam with the fish ladder.

Ask your parents or teachers if they have ever heard of fish ladders.

"Come on," said Mom, "let's go look at a Fish Ladder."

Fish climbing ladders? Even I know they don't have hands and feet. "What is a fish ladder, Mom?" I asked.

"Climb over here, Spenser," she said, "and look down at the Columbia River. That big thing in the middle of the river is the Bonneville Dam. See how high it is? Well, the poor fish can't swim that high so they need a little help getting up and over the dam. The ladder helps them to make their way up and over."

"Pretty cool," I thought, pictures of fish climbing ladders still in my head.

"Kids Kowstruction"
sculpture by Chris Keylock Williams
at the Portland Children's Museum

Lewis and Clark Mural
Portland Historical Society Building

Can you describe a rose? Have you ever seen one? If you have, give yourself a point. If you haven't seen a rose, go look next time you are at the grocery store. Then you can give yourself a point.

People

Mom and I love to meet people, and the people of Portland are some of the very best!

Art, dance, music – Portland has plenty of the arts – but the one thing Mom wants me to see are the roses! Portland is famous for its roses.

"Spenser, did you know that Portland is called the City of Roses? And every year they have a big celebration called the Portland Rose Festival with parades and concerts and fireworks," Mom told me.

Have you seen a rose? They are very pretty and smell so sweet. What is your favorite color for a rose? My favorite is yellow.

"Why roses, Mom?" I asked.

"In the early years of Portland," Mom said, "a lady set up a tent in her garden and invited people to come display their roses. That was the first Portland Rose Show. Soon they planted roses all along the streets to welcome visitors. Roses love the climate in Portland – warm in the summer and not too cold in the winter. There is also a very large rose garden where they try to grow different kinds of roses."

"Wow," I thought, "no wonder Portland is such a pretty city."

Tidbit

The rose is a symbol of love and beauty, which is why we give so many of them on Valentine's Day. The rose is the national flower of the United States.

Lending a Paw

"Operation Hungry Child" is what Mom calls her pet project. She says she named it for me because I am always hungry, but I know she named it for the hungry children that are found in every city in America. Mom and I will keep working until all hungry children are fed. And you can help us.

In each city we visit, we take time to find someone who is feeding children and we offer to help. In Portland there is Oregon Food Bank. Oregon Food Bank collects food and gives it to places that help children who are hungry all across the region.

You should talk to your parents about what you can do to help others. Once you do, give yourself a point.

Tidbit

Can you imagine going to bed at night with a hungry stomach? Many children do – in this country and all over the world.

"Come along, Spenser," Mom says. And we are off to sort huge boxes of food. Today we are sorting potatoes, so Mom and I put on our gloves and get to work.

Have you helped your parents do something good for someone else? Hunger is our special project, but there are lots of people that need help every day. Just because we are kids (and dogs), it doesn't mean we can't do our share to help.

You can write to me at spensernation.com, my website, and tell me your ideas. Then I can share them with other children. If we all work together helping people, we can fix lots of problems.

"Bountiful Harvest"
Mural by Mary Josephson
Oregon Food Bank

Tidbit

There are many things that children can do to help people. Saving your allowance and giving it to a good cause, visiting an older person, or playing with a child who doesn't have a friend are some examples.

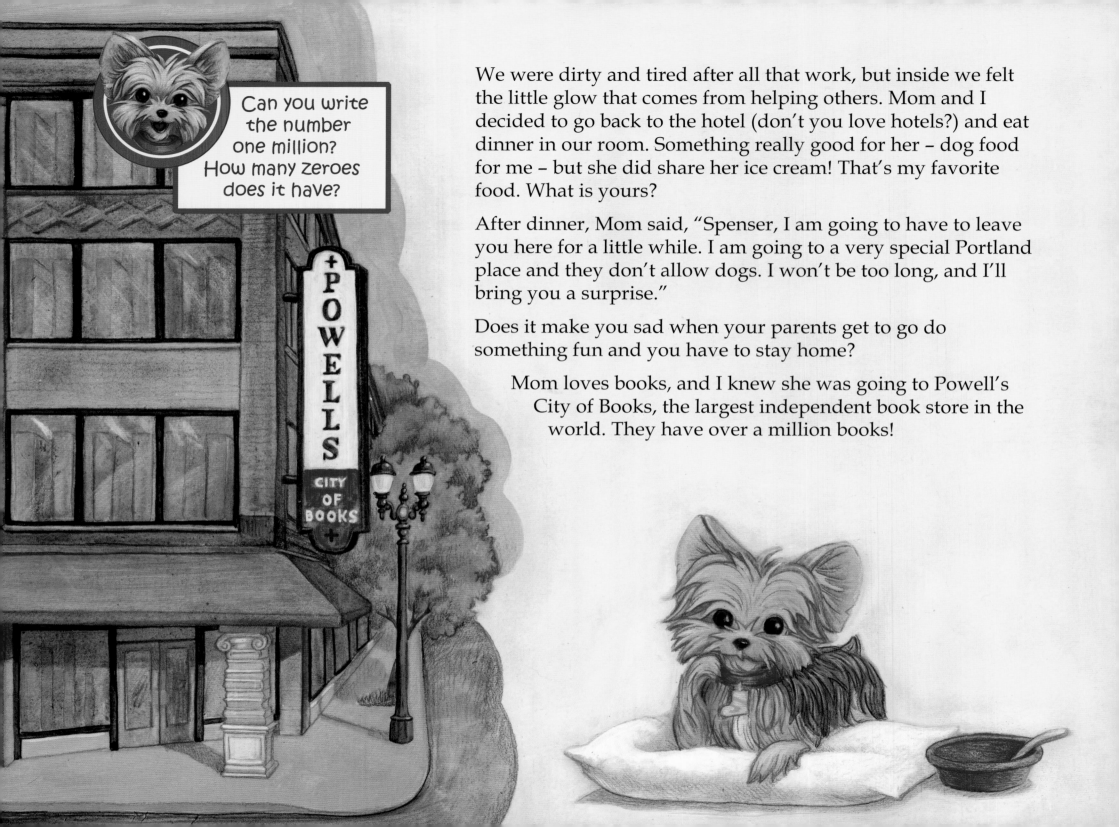

Can you write the number one million? How many zeroes does it have?

We were dirty and tired after all that work, but inside we felt the little glow that comes from helping others. Mom and I decided to go back to the hotel (don't you love hotels?) and eat dinner in our room. Something really good for her – dog food for me – but she did share her ice cream! That's my favorite food. What is yours?

After dinner, Mom said, "Spenser, I am going to have to leave you here for a little while. I am going to a very special Portland place and they don't allow dogs. I won't be too long, and I'll bring you a surprise."

Does it make you sad when your parents get to go do something fun and you have to stay home?

Mom loves books, and I knew she was going to Powell's City of Books, the largest independent book store in the world. They have over a million books!

Mom did come back before too long and she brought me a
new storybook. I love reading! Mom and I snuggled down and
rested our tired bodies while we read my new story. My eyes
closed tight and I was sound asleep. Our trip was almost over.
Tomorrow we would leave for home.

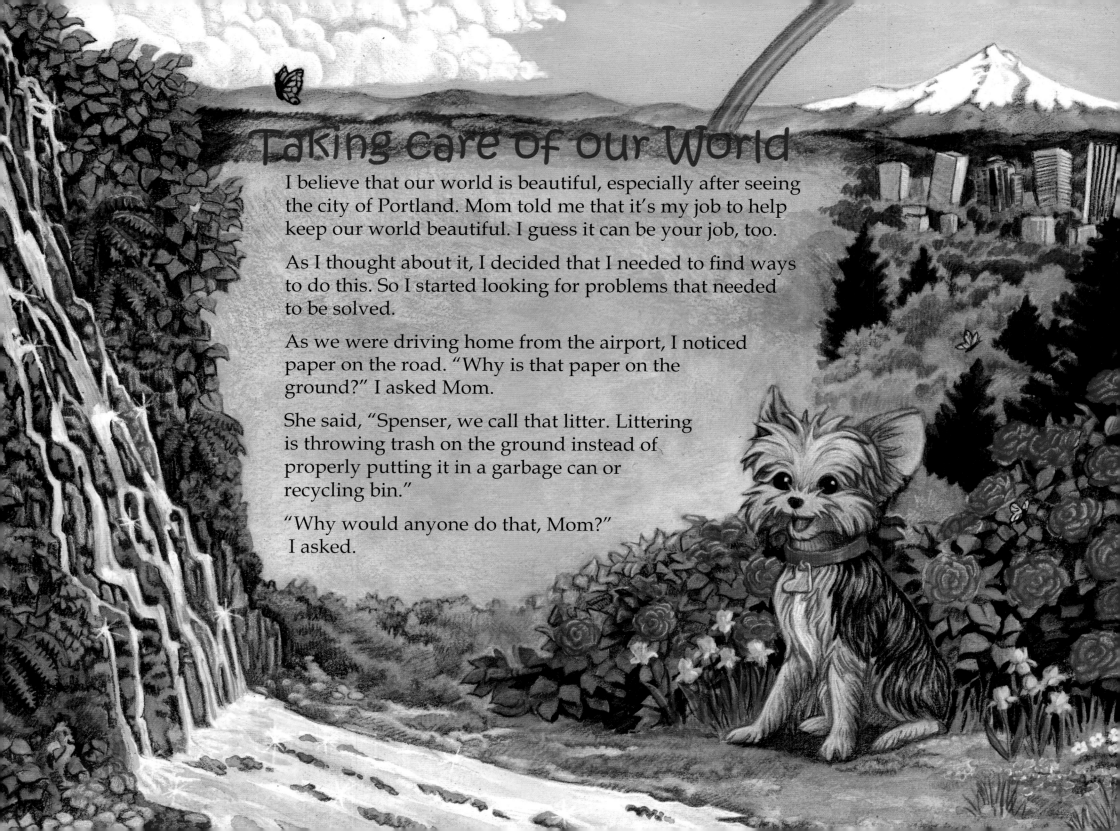

Taking Care of our World

I believe that our world is beautiful, especially after seeing the city of Portland. Mom told me that it's my job to help keep our world beautiful. I guess it can be your job, too.

As I thought about it, I decided that I needed to find ways to do this. So I started looking for problems that needed to be solved.

As we were driving home from the airport, I noticed paper on the road. "Why is that paper on the ground?" I asked Mom.

She said, "Spenser, we call that litter. Littering is throwing trash on the ground instead of properly putting it in a garbage can or recycling bin."

"Why would anyone do that, Mom?" I asked.

"I don't know, Spenser," Mom said, "but it is a very big problem for our world." My ears pricked up – a problem? Well, I was looking for a problem.

"Can I do anything to help with littering?" I asked Mom.

"Yes, Spenser, you can always put your trash where it belongs. You can talk to other children at school, at church, even when you play, and tell them how important it is to put trash where it belongs."

And so, I'm going to work on this. If you would like to help me, talk to your parents or your teachers and see how you can help, too. Write me and tell me what you decide. Together we can make a big difference!

Tidbit

A piece of gum thrown out of the car window can be very dangerous to a bird that tries to eat it.

Tidbit

We were back at home. My suitcase was on the shelf and my raincoat and boots were in the closet. I would never wear them again without thinking of the big waterfall in Portland. Mom and I had finished another excellent adventure.

As she tucked me into my bed, she held me close, kissed my head, and said, "Thanks, Spenser, for taking this wonderful trip with me, exploring our world and taking care of our friends. This is why we are here - to take care of each other and to take care of our world. It is especially fun when we can explore and learn about new places together. I can't wait until next time."

"Me, too," I thought as I drifted off to sleep, "Thanks, Mom, for sharing this trip with me. I'm ready to go somewhere new anytime you are ready."

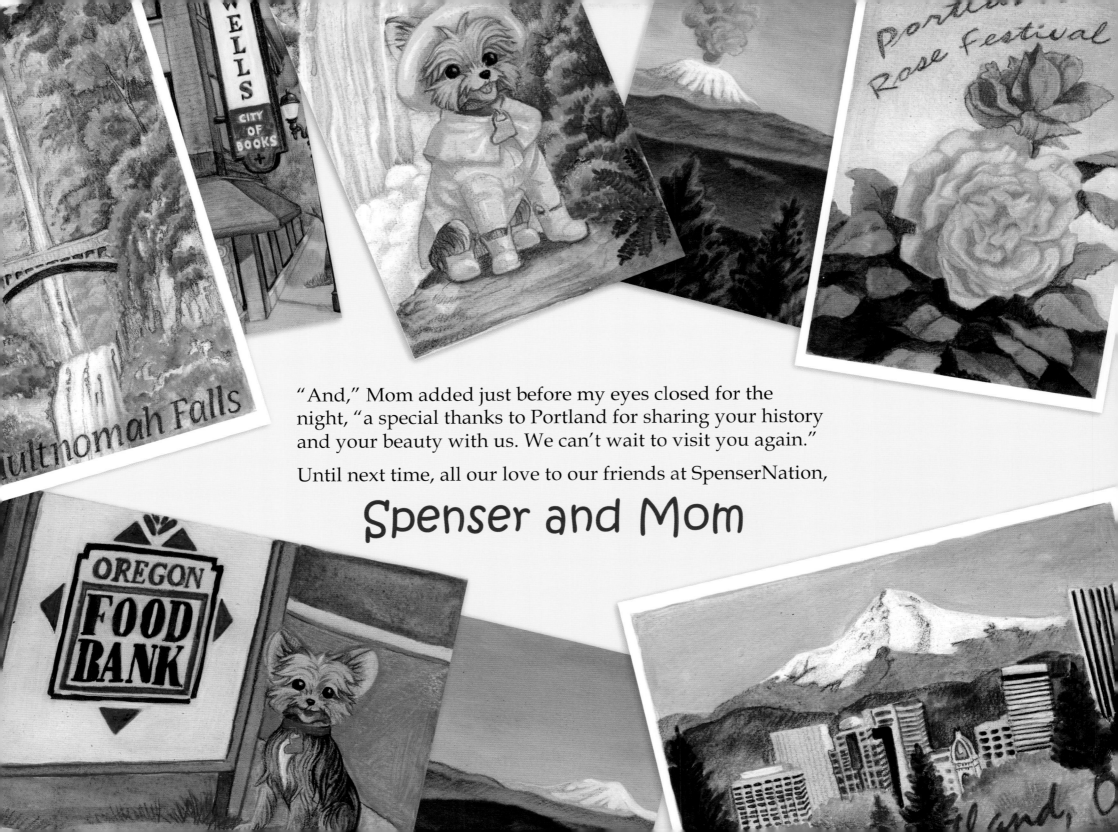

"And," Mom added just before my eyes closed for the night, "a special thanks to Portland for sharing your history and your beauty with us. We can't wait to visit you again."

Until next time, all our love to our friends at SpenserNation,

Spenser and Mom

Spenser Nation.com

Visit my website, www.spensernation.com to email me, send me your pictures, look at my photo album, and other fun things.

🦴 Moms and Dads may want to check for suggestions for family activities on the Parents tab.

🦴 More information for educators, including free teaching guides, can be found on the Teachers tab. Guides are designed for pre-kindergarten through second grade and include subjects – Math, Science, Language Arts, Social Studies, and Fine Arts.

🦴 Watch for other Spenser and Mom books as we continue to explore this great country. Visits are planned for St. Louis, El Paso, and Philadelphia in the near future.

What other cities or areas do you think I should visit?

Your traveling pal,

 Spenser

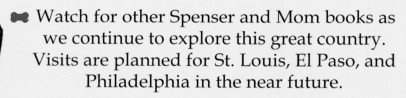

About Oregon Food Bank

Oregon Food Bank recovers food from farmers, manufacturers, wholesalers, retailers, individuals and government sources and distributes it fairly and equitably throughout a statewide network of 20 regional food banks and 919 local hunger-relief agencies throughout Oregon and Clark County, Wash.

In addition, OFB works to eliminate the root causes of hunger through advocacy, nutrition education, learning gardens and public education.

Facts About Hunger

◆ Hunger isn't just uncomfortable for kids, it's dangerous.

◆ Hunger jeopardizes a child's health, development and future productivity.

◆ Every month, 71,000 Oregon children eat meals from an emergency food box.

Oregon Food Bank's mission is to eliminate hunger and its root causes ... because no one should be hungry.